SCHOOL STINKS!

SCHOOL STINKS!

**Judith Ross Enderle
and Stephanie Jacob Gordon**

SCHOLASTIC INC.
New York Toronto London Auckland Sydney
Mexico City New Delhi Hong Kong Buenos Aires

ISBN 0-439-32852-7

12 11 10 9 8 7 6 5 4   4 5 6/0

Printed in the U.S.A.   40
First Scholastic printing, October 2001

Table of Contents

Chapter One —
School Really, Really Stinks 1
Chapter Two —
Tuna Surprise Really Stinks 11
Chapter Three —
The Kool Duds Kid 20
Chapter Four —
A Not-so-empty Field 29
Chapter Five —
A Not-quite-so-stinky Day in
Third Grade 44
Chapter Six —
Oh, Oh, Flapjack 54
Chapter Seven —
Flora's Club 68
Chapter Eight —
The First Meeting 78
Chapter Nine —
Moving Day 88
Chapter Ten —
The New People 101
Chapter Eleven —
D-U-M-B 107

Chapter Twelve —
   Sam, Kate, and *Three*   117
Chapter Thirteen —
   Not One Freckle   126
Chapter Fourteen —
   How Many Freckles?   138

SCHOOL STINKS!

Chapter One
School Really, Really Stinks

School really, really, really stinks because . . . Flora wrote in her GOOD Things-BAD Things notebook. Next to her name she drew a daisy. She always drew flowers by her name. Her name meant flower. She loved her name. But today that was all she loved.

1) BAD — Max Bloom, the only person I know in this whole school, is in Mr. Crane's class. I'm not!

2) BAD — I don't know anyone in Mrs. Lee's class.

3) BAD — I'm sitting in the front row.

4) BAD — Hot lunch is tuna fish surprise. I hate tuna fish. It's not a good surprise.

5) BAD — There are no GOOD things in third grade.

"We'll start with you, Flora Ann Cole," said Mrs. Lee.

Flora looked up. Start what? She hadn't been listening.

"In third grade, we have to use our ears," said Mrs. Lee. She had a skinny smile. She wrote something in her teacher's book.

She's probably giving me an F in listening, Flora thought. My first day in third grade and I'm already in trouble. Mom and Dad wouldn't like that. I'll probably be grounded. I'll probably be in third grade again next year.

"Flora?" said Mrs. Lee.

"Yes," said Flora. She sat up straight. She tried to put a listening look on her face.

"Flora, stand up and tell us something about yourself," said the teacher.

Flora jumped up. Her knees felt wobbly. Her face was hot. "I . . . um . . . moved to Tower Road in the summer. I take piano lessons. But mostly, I like to make up plays." Flora sat down as fast as she could.

"Welcome to Poplar Elementary, Flora," said Mrs. Lee. Her smile was still skinny. "We hope you'll share one of your plays with us." She called on the next person.

No one else was new. No one else said they liked plays. Mrs. Lee didn't tell any other kids to use their ears.

Flora raised her hand. She hoped Mrs. Lee would let her pass out the new books. But she didn't. Flora loved new reading books and new workbooks. New books always smelled good. She liked the way the pages were smooth, with no pencil marks or fingerprints. She wrote her name in neat handwriting inside her workbook. Meg, across the aisle, was printing her name, just like a second grader.

Mrs. Lee talked a lot. In her class, there were a zillion rules. It was hard to keep listening. Flora wished they would get to the third-grade stuff. It seemed the whole morning was filled up with talking.

Just before lunch, Mrs. Lee said, "Line up, everyone. We're going to the library."

Flora was first in line. At last, they were doing something she liked.

The class marched down the hall. "Don't you just love the library?" Flora whispered to Kate, who walked with Meg and Josie. Kate sat in the third row in front. Kate wore glasses. Flora wondered if she liked to read.

Kate didn't answer. She whispered to Josie.

Josie had curly hair like Flora, but her hair was red. "Flora's new, Kate," Josie said. "She didn't know you like to be line leader."

"She knows now," said Meg, who had stick-up black hair and butterfly earrings.

"Girls, move along. No talking in the halls," said Mrs. Lee.

Kate glanced at Flora. Flora looked at Kate. She knew Kate was

5

waiting for her to move behind her. Well, she wouldn't. Kate was like Sienna at her old school. She always had to be first, too. Flora walked faster and stayed close to Mrs. Lee. She didn't care about being line leader. She just wanted to get to the library.

Flora missed her old school. She missed her old friends. Who would be her friend at this new school? Probably not Kate.

Kate, Meg, and Josie whispered all the way down the hall. Flora ignored them. That's what her mom said to do when people bothered you. Flora couldn't always do it. But this time she could.

The library was perfect. There were bunches and bunches of books on shelves. There was a whole rack of magazines. Posters hung on colored yarn from the ceiling. There was a bulletin board of new book covers. There were baskets of stuffed animals. There was a puzzle table and a computer desk. Three beanbag chairs and a rocker were in the corner.

The class sat in a circle in front of the rocker. Josie and Meg plopped into beanbags. Flora snuggled into the third one, the blue one.

Kate said, "Now you're in my seat." She put her hands on her hips. Her eyes looked angry behind her glasses.

"Uh-uh," said Flora. She snuggled in deeper and folded her arms.

"We always sit in the beanbags," said Josie.

"We're best friends. We do everything together," said Meg. "You have to let Kate sit there."

"No I don't," said Flora.

"Girls," said Mrs. Lee. "Our librar-

ian, Mr. Robb, is waiting for us. Kate, please sit down."

Meg and Josie inched their bean-bags away from Flora. Kate sat really close to them. They started talking about their favorite books.

Flora wished she could tell some-one about her favorite books. She wished she could sit close to someone, too. But definitely not Kate.

Mr. Robb sat in the rocking chair. He wore a yellow bow tie with green polka dots. He looked very nice. "We have some new books in our library this year," he said. "Explore the shelves to find them. Third graders may check out books before and after school as well as during library time. Come visit me often," he said.

Flora couldn't wait to check out books. She couldn't wait to write in her GOOD-BAD notebook.

6) GOOD — I love the library!

The library didn't stink even a little. But some people who wanted beanbags did! Flora sighed. Should she make that number seven in her book?

Chapter Two
Tuna Surprise
Really Stinks

The cafeteria was also the auditorium. And it was the gym. Long folding tables were lined up on the wood floor. There were lots of tall trash cans. The room smelled yucky, all fishy and steamy.

Flora got in the hot lunch line. Her mom had thought hot lunch would be a treat. Flora would rather have had a pbj and an apple.

She tried not to look at the plate of tuna surprise on her tray. She tried not to smell it, either. Where should she sit? Everyone seemed to know everyone else. She didn't know anyone, except Max, who lived next door to her, and some people she didn't want to know. And they knew who they were. She started toward Max's table. But only boys were sitting there. So she changed her mind. Her fingers ached from holding her tray.

"Find a seat, please," said a lunchroom mom. She pointed to the table where Kate, Meg, and Josie were sitting. Flora hesitated. "Go on," said the lunchroom mom.

Her mom always said not to judge right away. Her mom always said to give people a chance. Okay. She'd give Kate, Meg, and Josie one more chance to be nice. One more. That was all. Flora squeezed in on the end of the bench.

"I hate tuna surprise," said Kate.

"Me, too," said Meg.

"Me, too," said Josie.

"Me, too," said Flora.

"And I hate people who take my beanbag chair," said Kate. "And my place in line."

Everyone looked at Flora. Flora looked at her tray. Some people didn't deserve another chance, she thought.

"My mom says not to hate people. You can hate what they do, though," said Josie.

"Your mom always says stuff," said Kate.

"Oh, my mom always says stuff, too," said Flora. Maybe she and Josie could be friends. She smiled at Josie. But Josie didn't smile back.

Suddenly Kate scraped her plate onto Meg's. Everyone laughed.

Meg scraped her plate onto Josie's plate, even while Josie tried to cover her plate. She got tuna surprise all over her hands.

Josie looked at Flora. Flora looked back.

"Oh, look at those silly boys," said Kate.

Flora looked. She didn't see what boys Kate meant. She turned back to find her plate heaped with tuna surprise.

The other girls laughed. Josie was wiping her hands on a napkin.

"We're done," said Kate. She, Josie, and Meg left the table.

Flora stared at the mountain of tuna surprise. She couldn't throw it out. There was an older kid who was waste-can monitor. She'd get reported. Flora's stomach churned. Tuna surprise stunk worse than all the other stuff in her GOOD-BAD notebook.

Kids were leaving for the playground. Pretty soon she'd be the only one in the lunchroom. Why were those girls so mean? She couldn't stop her tears. She felt like such a baby.

The lunchroom mom sat down beside her. "What's wrong, honey?" she asked.

"I can't — I can't eat all this," said Flora.

"Why did you ask for so much?" asked the mom.

"I — I didn't," Flora sobbed. Between her tears, she told what had happened.

"I'm sorry I didn't see it," said the mom. "Maybe tomorrow you'll make a new friend," she said.

This just made Flora cry harder.

The mom scooped up her tray. She

came back with an apple for Flora. "Go out on the playground now," she said.

"Thank you," whispered Flora. She wiped her eyes. She hoped her nose wasn't all red from crying. She hoped no one in her class had seen her being such a baby.

On the playground, Flora walked along the fence. Max was playing dodgeball with a group of boys. "Hi," she called.

Max didn't say hi back. He didn't even look at her. I guess he doesn't want to know me at school, Flora thought. She wished it were still summer. During the summer, he'd at least talked to her, as long as she didn't ask him to be in one of her plays. And he'd invited her over to see his pet spider.

The girls from lunch were playing hopscotch.

"Hey, Flora, want a surprise?" called Kate.

Flora kept walking. She wouldn't ever sit with those girls again. She wouldn't even talk to them. Not all year. Not next year. Not even when she was in junior high.

Flora found a bench under a tree. She thought about more things she would write in her GOOD-BAD notebook. By the time she was out of third grade, she would probably have ten million things under BAD. "Blech!" said Flora as the bell rang. "Third grade stinks."

Back in the classroom, Flora added to her BAD list. She had no doubts about it now:

7) BAD — The _MEANEST_ _MEANEST_ _MEANEST_ _MEANEST_ _MEANEST_ _MEANEST_ _MEANEST_ _MEANEST_ _MEANEST_ _MEANEST_

<u>(100 times MEANEST)</u> girls are in my class. Their names are —

The classroom had grown suddenly quiet — too quiet. Flora looked up. She hoped she hadn't been caught not using her ears again. Then she saw why no one was talking.

Chapter Three
The Kool Duds Kid

"Oh . . . oh . . . oh . . . look! It's the Kool Duds Kid," said Meg right out loud.

And it was. Flora would have known the girl from the TV ads anywhere. She was wearing purple jeans with the KD logo. And a purple-striped KD shirt. There was a purple KD scarf tucked into her back pocket, just like on TV. And a purple cap covered her curls. Even her earrings were little gold KDs. Flora couldn't stop staring. She'd never seen anyone in real life who was on TV.

"Third graders, we have another new student. This is Samantha Gold. Welcome to Poplar Elementary, Samantha," said Mrs. Lee. Now her smile wasn't so thin and all her teeth showed.

"Wel-come," singsonged the class.

The teacher pointed. "Meg, dear. Please move to the desk in the last row. Samantha, you may sit in Meg's desk. Flora is sitting across from you. She's a new student, too."

Samantha Gold didn't even look at Flora. She stared at Meg. Meg stared back. Then Meg pulled her things out of her desk. She stomped to the back of the room. Flora wondered if she should warn the new girl. Meg and her friends might be mean to Samantha for taking Meg's desk. But, at least, she hadn't taken Kate's desk. She was sure lucky about that.

21

"Tomorrow," said Mrs. Lee, "we will start our third-grade writing project. Our class will publish a magazine. Think about what you would like to do for the project. Bring your ideas to school."

Flora raised her hand. Mrs. Lee called on her. "Do you mean ideas like how to put it together? Like writing stories? Or poems? Like making ads?" she asked.

"That's right, Flora. All of those."

"I want to do all of it," said Flora.

Mrs. Lee smiled. "We'll be choosing teams. You'll work together," she said.

Flora leaned toward Samantha. "Want to be on a team with me?" she asked.

Samantha shrugged. "Maybe," she said. "And maybe not."

Flora shrugged, too. Samantha Gold didn't like her, either. No one did.

Third grade really stinks, she thought. She added to her list.

8) BAD — No one wants to be my friend. Not even the other new girl.

After the math review, the class practiced handwriting. Flora wasn't too good in math. She did better in handwriting. Most of the other kids were just starting cursive letters at this school. Mrs. Lee wrote GOOD. She drew a happy face on the top of Flora's paper. Two GOOD things and ten billion BADS, Flora thought.

But maybe third grade wouldn't stink so much tomorrow. Maybe after they finished the magazine, Mrs. Lee would want to put on a play. Maybe she'd let Flora write the play. Maybe . . . Flora could think of a zillion maybe's.

The going-home bell rang.

Kate and Meg and Josie crowded around Samantha's desk. They acted like she was a famous movie star.

"Want to be on our team for the writing project?" asked Kate.

Meg hung back.

"You could write about being the Kool Duds Kid," said Josie. "Like how it feels to be famous."

Samantha shrugged. "I don't think so," she said.

"Why not?" asked Kate.

"Why should I?" asked Samantha. She slid out of her seat. She squeezed past them and out the door.

"Oh, she's so-o-o stuck-up," said Kate. She pushed her nose up with her finger. "I'm the Kool Duds Kid and you're not," she said.

"I told you," said Meg.

Kate turned toward Flora. "Too bad. You have to sit by her. Boy, are you going to hate that."

Flora wasn't sure what to say. Samantha hadn't been exactly friendly. But she hadn't been mean, like Kate and her friends. "Maybe," said Flora. "And maybe not."

"What's that supposed to mean?" asked Meg.

"I don't even know her," said Flora. "How do I know if she's stuck-up? How can you say what she's like? It's only the *first* day of third grade." Then she remembered. She wasn't going to talk to these girls. Not ever. Now it was too late.

"Yeah," said Josie. "Maybe tomorrow we can make friends with Samantha."

"Yeah," said Meg. "And maybe we'll get to be in a Kool Duds ad on TV."

Kate glared at Flora. "I don't think

so," she said. She sounded just like Samantha. "Samantha Gold thinks she's so-o-o special, she can take anybody's desk. Big deal she's the Kool Duds Kid. Big deal she's on TV. Big deal!" Kate headed for the door with Meg and Josie following.

Flora sighed. If she were a Kool Duds Kid, Josie and Meg would want to be her friend. But she was just Flora Ann Cole. She was really good at making up plays. But she wasn't famous for anything.

On the school bus, Max sat across from Flora. "Mr. Crane's class is great," he said. "We had art first thing. And I sit in the very back. It's the best!"

"We're starting a writing project tomorrow," said Flora.

"I told you I was in the best class," said Max. "We don't have to write

27

anything!" He gave the boy beside him a high five.

Flora slid down in her seat. She wouldn't let Max or anyone know how much she hated her class. Why did school have to stink so much?

Chapter Four
A Not-so-empty Field

At home, Flora changed out of her school clothes. Since she didn't have any homework to do, she practiced her piano music. Flora liked playing the piano. Someday she wanted to be good enough to play the piano in a famous orchestra. Piano definitely went under GOOD in her GOOD-BAD notebook.

After practicing, she went to her room to find the book she was reading. Her little sister, Polly, bounced on her bed. "And then in my kindergarten, we sang a song with my name, a Polly Doodle song," she said. "And then . . ."

Their dog, Flapjack, bounced, too. Flapjack was a wirehaired terrier. He was really cute. He had white wiggly fur with gray spots, and he felt like a pot scrubber when Flora scratched him. He was really smart, too, and good at kissing. And nothing ever bothered Flapjack when he wanted to sleep. He liked to sleep on Polly's bed — even when she was bouncing.

Flora didn't want to hear one more word about Polly's wonderful kindergarten. She looked out the window. Max and some boys from school were playing in front of Max's house. And at the end of the street, where the field used to be . . . Flora looked really hard. At last! "I can't talk now," she said. "I have to go."

During the summer, someone had built a house in the field at the end of Tower Road. First had come the hole for the basement. Then the loads of cinder blocks and the cement trucks. Then the piles of lumber and lots of banging and loud music while the carpenters worked. Soon there was a roof and an outside. When the inside was finished, the gardeners came. Grass and flowers and trees grew in just one day.

This house was the biggest of all the houses on Tower Road. In fact, this was the biggest house Flora had ever seen.

Then the FOR SALE sign went up.

"Come on, Max," Flora called as she raced out the front door.

"Why?" he yelled.

"Who's she?" asked one of the other boys.

31

"Max has a girlfriend," called another.

"Do not," he said.

The other boys laughed and teased.

"Let's go inside," said Max. "My mom bought some cookies."

The boys ran after Max.

"Didn't you see? The new house has a SOLD sign on it," called Flora. But they didn't even look back. She plopped down on the curb. Boys can be very difficult, she decided.

"When are the new people coming?" she asked in a deep voice, like her dad. She smoothed her hair back and smiled until she was sure she looked like her mom. "I don't know," said Flora in a mom voice. "I hope it's a nice family. I hope they have a lot of girls." She sighed. Playacting by yourself wasn't much fun. But she couldn't wait for the new family to move in. Her family was the last new family on Tower Road. They'd lived there the whole summer before third grade.

"My mom says someone will move in soon. And she says they'll be rich, because they bought such a big house." Max was coming across her front yard. Flora guessed the other boys had gone home, though she hadn't seen them leave. He pulled a yo-yo out of his pocket. He made the yo-yo sleep before it zipped back up into his hand.

Flora had a bright pink yo-yo, but she was tired of it. Polly had tangled the string. Now Flora couldn't get the knots out.

"But how soon?" asked Flora. If soon was tomorrow, they might have someone new to play with. Someone who might like to act in plays. Max had said, "Yuck!" when she'd asked him, even though she'd offered to let him be a pirate. And Polly was too little. She only wanted to be a dancer or a singer or someone who wore a glittery costume.

Max shrugged. "My mom didn't know."

"Do they have kids?" asked Flora. Max's mom sold plastic kitchen stuff and cosmetics and baskets. She knew about every house on Tower Road.

"Mom's friend at the real estate place said they have a kid named Sam," said Max.

"Oh," said Flora, hugging her knees.

"Sam might be big, like my brother, Kurt." He zipped his yo-yo straight out in front of him.

"Sam might be in third grade, like us," said Flora. She'd hoped for a girl.

Boys were okay, but they weren't girls. "So, what do you want to do now?" she asked.

"Let's have a yo-yo contest," said Max.

"No, something different," said Flora. "I know. Let's have a club."

"What kind of club?" asked Max.

"How about a Reading Club?" said Flora. "Our class went to the library at school. Third graders can take out books. We could read together."

Max groaned. "You always want to do dumb things. We should have a Sports Club."

Flora groaned just as loud as Max. "No way," she said. "How about a Making Things Club?"

"What kind of things?" asked Max.

"I have a paint set and crayons and paper and glitter glue and scissors. And I have a really, really neat bracelet kit that my grandma gave me," said Flora.

"Bracelets! Ee-yew," said Max. "NO WAY!"

Flora sighed. She knew it. Boys never wanted to do anything fun. She wouldn't even mention her idea for a Plays Club. She could guess what he'd say about that.

"Forget clubs," said Max, winding up his yo-yo string. "I have to go home. I've got a new tarantula. His name is Lucky."

"Why did you name him that?" asked Flora.

"Because he's lucky he's mine," said Max, laughing. He ran toward his house.

That's another thing about boys, Flora thought. Just when you are about to have a club, they want to play with their pets. She'd never have a spider for a pet. What did spiders eat, anyway? Other bugs, she thought. Yuck! She hugged her knees. If only a girl would move in on Tower Road. . . .

"Whatcha doing?" Polly plopped down on the curb beside Flora. "Want me to sing my Polly Doodle song for you now?"

"NO! I'm busy wishing," Flora said. She wasn't in the mood to explain stuff to Polly.

"I'll wish, too. What are you wishing for?" Polly tapped Flora's arm. "Tell me. Please. And I'll tell you my wish."

"If I tell you, the wish won't come true," said Flora. She inched away from Polly.

Polly moved closer again. "I can tell you my wish. It will come true even if you know it."

"Well, mine won't." Flora's wish

wouldn't come true anyway. She knew who was moving in.

"I wish . . . I wish . . . Never mind," said Polly. "I'm not going to tell you, either." She jumped up. With both arms out, she tiptoed along the curb. "I'm a famous tightrope walker," she said. "I have a sparkly red suit on. I am very beautiful."

Flora sighed. What a show-off, she thought.

"Flora, Polly," Mom called from the front porch. "Time to wash up for dinner and set the table."

"Race you," said Polly. Her ponytail bobbled as she ran ahead.

Flora trailed slowly. If only she could think of a good club, then it might not matter that third-grade girls were so stinky. She would have fun at home, even if she did have only Max and the new boy, Sam, to play with. But it wouldn't be a Sports Club. And it wouldn't be a Reading Club. She really needed a girl to be her friend. Then they could have a Girls Only Club. But Polly was the only other girl on Tower Road. And Flora didn't want to have a club with her kindergarten baby sister.

Dad pulled into the drive as Flora started up the front steps. She waited for him. Dad was the only boy she really, really liked. He never thought reading was dumb. He liked to watch her plays. Sometimes he even acted in them. And he never wanted to play sports or feed spiders more than anything else.

"Hi, Flora Belle. How's my pretty posy?" Dad asked.

"Oh, Daddy! Why do so many boys live on this street?" she asked.

"Since when is two so many? Or did Mrs. Bloom adopt a football team when I wasn't looking?" He gave Flora a hug.

But Flora didn't feel huggy. She felt grouchy. "Daddy! Two boys is too many. And Max says the people who bought the new house have a boy, too."

Her dad winked. "Boys are pretty good guys when you give them a chance. I'm a boy and your mom likes me." He put his briefcase by the door. "So, how do you like third grade, Flora Belle?"

Flora shrugged. "It's okay, I guess." She didn't want to explain how stinky it really was. "There's only one other new kid."

"Oh, you won't be new forever," said Dad.

Flora wasn't so sure. She might be the first kid ever to be new for a whole year in third grade.

Flora could smell spaghetti sauce. Spaghetti was her second favorite food. Her first was chocolate ice cream. She ran to help set the table.

After dinner and after the dishes, Flora started upstairs. Polly ran up behind her. "Flora Dora Mora, I'm going to tell you my wish now," said Polly. "It will come true, even if I tell. I know it. I wish that a little girl would move into the new house."

Flora stopped at the landing. She turned to face Polly. "Don't call me Dora Mora! And your wish won't come true. Because the only kid moving into the new house is Sam. Sam. Sam. Sam. A boy." She said it in a mean voice, as if she were glad that

Polly's wish wouldn't come true. But she wasn't.

Polly squeezed past Flora. She skipped toward their room. "So?" she said. "In my kindergarten, there's a girl named Bobi. Sam could be a girl. My wish could still come true. Sam is a girl who's five and in kindergarten, just like me. She will be my bestest friend. Bester than anything."

"Bestest and bester aren't words," said Flora. She walked slowly down the hall. Sam could be a girl. But Sam wouldn't be. Sam would be a boy. And it didn't matter. Flora didn't care. She'd just act in all her plays by herself. She'd be her own bestest friend, bester than anybody. "Blech!"

Chapter Five
A Not-quite-so-stinky Day in Third Grade

The Kool Duds Kid was absent from school the next day. Kate was really upset. She had worn her Kool Duds outfit to school.

That morning Mrs. Lee explained the different parts of a magazine. She showed them lots of magazines. Then she assigned everyone to a team. There were article teams, story teams, and an advertising team. Flora was teamed with Josie and a boy named Trang. They were the ad team. Flora had hoped that she would be able to write stories or articles. She didn't want to write ads. But Mrs. Lee said there would be no changes.

"What about the Kool Duds Kid?" asked Josie. "Can she be on our team?"

The teacher said that Samantha would be on Kate's team along with Adam.

"But I want Kate on my team," said Meg, who was teamed with two boys. Kate, Meg, and Josie all looked upset.

Then Kate raised her hand again. "Can't Meg and Josie and I pleeee-ase be on the same team?" she asked. "Last year, we did everything to-gether."

"This is this year," said Mrs. Lee. "I said there would be no changes. You'll have three weeks to complete this project. Now get together with your teammates. The writing teams discuss topics. The ad teams must create six ads — two full-page ads, three smaller space ads, and a page of classifieds. Each ad should be for a different product or service. Don't forget to include artwork."

Trang and Flora pulled their desks close. Josie sat a little ways apart.

"Ads will be easy," said Trang. "We are lucky. Let's write ads for computer games."

"We'll need more. I vote for a bookstore ad," Flora said.

"It could be the other large ad," said Trang. "If we each take two things, then we'll have it all done."

"Well, I'm not doing the classified ads," said Josie.

"I'll write the classifieds," said Flora. "What ads do you want to do, Josie?"

Josie scrunched up her face as if she were thinking really hard. "Well . . . I go to tap-dancing class and I could . . ."

"So does my sister. She goes to the Little Swan Dance School," said Flora.

"I went there when I was little," said Josie. "Now I go to Grand Academy of Dance."

"Then you do two of the small space ads, Josie," Trang said. "One could be for the dance school."

"And the other one will be for collector dolls. I have five already. I'm going to get the cowgirl doll for my birthday. Do you like dolls?" she asked.

"Me?" asked Trang. "No way!"

Josie and Flora both laughed.

"I meant Flora, silly," said Josie.

"I like dolls okay," said Flora. "I like books and plays and making stuff." Oops! She'd talked to Josie. Well, Josie had talked to her first. And she seemed nicer than Kate and Meg. Maybe she'd talk to Josie only when Kate and Meg weren't around.

"How are you doing?" asked Mrs. Lee, stopping by their circle.

"I'm doing one large ad and the classifieds," said Flora.

"I'm doing one small ad and one big ad," said Trang.

"I'm doing the rest," said Josie.

"I'm glad to see that you are working together so well," said Mrs. Lee. "Keep it up." This time she smiled a real smile. Flora wished the teacher would smile all the time. She looked so nice when she smiled.

Mrs. Lee moved to the next group.

"All right, students. We are finished planning now," said Mrs. Lee a few minutes later. "Put your desks

back in order. Before you take out your math workbooks, we have to choose a name for our magazine. I'll write your ideas on the board. Then we will vote."

At first, no one raised his or her hand. Then Adam suggested, *"Poplar Magazine."*

Flora raised her hand. *"Third,"* she said, "for third grade."

Trang said, "I like Flora's idea. But I think *Three* sounds better."

Other ideas were: *Fun Magazine, Third-grade Friends,* and WOW.

Then everyone voted.

"Three is the name of our new magazine," said Mrs. Lee.

Flora turned around and smiled at Trang. She felt as if the title were partly hers. He gave her a thumbs-up. She liked Trang. Maybe she would have another boy for a friend. And maybe Josie would be her friend, too. Now she couldn't wait to get started on her ads.

At noon, Flora walked to the lunchroom with Josie. At the door, Kate ran up to them. "Don't you just hate that stupid magazine project? It's the dumbest thing we ever had to do. Don't you think?"

"Our group is fun," said Josie. "Isn't it?" She turned to Flora.

"It's real fun," said Flora. "What are you doing in your group?" It was impossible not to talk to Kate and her friends.

"None of your beeswax," said Kate. "Come on, Josie. Let's find Meg."

"Come on, Flora," said Josie.

"I didn't say she could come," said Kate.

"Oh," said Josie.

"Now you like Flora better than me," said Kate. She stomped away.

"She won't stay mad," said Josie.

"Why doesn't she like me?" asked Flora.

Josie shrugged. "When Kate does things that make me mad, my mom says, 'She doesn't mean anything. That's just how Kate is right now.' Try not to be mad at her, Flora."

"Why? She's always mean to me," said Flora.

"She used to be really nice. It's just that . . . I mean, my mom says . . . Come on, let's see what they have for lunch today," said Josie.

"What does your mom say about Kate?" Flora asked.

"Never mind. I'm not supposed to tell," said Josie.

No matter how hard she tried,

Flora couldn't get Josie to tell her about Kate. Still, Flora was happy. No tuna surprise today. Flora loved pizza!

Later on the bus, Flora started a list for her classified ads.

She had a ton of homework. Tonight she would barely have time to work on her GOOD-BAD list. And tonight she finally had something else GOOD to write in her notebook.

Chapter Six
Oh, Oh,
Flapjack

Flora hated Dad's new computer game. Computer soccer! Polly loved it. Polly played it even before she was ready for school. And she was playing it now after school. Flora didn't care. She sat at the piano practicing her favorite piece by Mozart.

Mom called from the kitchen. "Polly, come pick up your toys. Flora, have you seen Flapjack?"

"No," Flora answered. "I'll look for him." First she checked all the bedrooms. Then she looked on the chairs and the couch. She even looked under the tables. She couldn't find Flapjack anywhere. Finally she ran outside.

"Flapjack!" Flora called.

She looked in the garage. No Flapjack. She looked in the backyard. No Flapjack. She looked up and down the street. Still no Flapjack. Flora looked both ways. Then she crossed the street.

The windows on the new house still had stickers on the glass. The front door was propped open. Maybe someone had moved in!

Then, through the big front window, Flora spotted Flapjack. He was inside the new house! "Flapjack! Come!" Flora called. "Hurry! Right now! Here, boy." But her dog didn't come out of the house.

Flora knew she wasn't supposed to go inside. From the moment the first tractor had arrived at the vacant lot, her mom and dad had been clear about that. She and Polly were never to go near the construction. Not even if Max went. Not even if the construction workers said it was okay. They could watch from the curb in front of their house. But they were never to go into the new house.

"Flapjack, please, please, please, come out," Flora pleaded. Flapjack still didn't come.

She peeked in the door. The new house smelled like paint. She listened. *Click, click, click.* Flapjack's toenails tapped on the bare floor. "You are in big trouble, Flapjack," Flora called. Her voice echoed.

She tiptoed inside the new house. There was no furniture. The new people aren't here yet, she thought. Flora tiptoed across the living room

and past the new kitchen. This could be a play, she thought. I could be the secret agent on the trail of the bad guy and his dog.

She listened for her dog and heard the faint *click click* again. It sounded as if it were coming from upstairs. The wood floors in the new house were as shiny as mirrors, not like the floors at Flora's house. "This is the most gigantic house I have been in . . . ever!" said Flora. Her voice echoed and it startled her. "Ssssh," she whispered as she started up the wide staircase.

At the top, Flora stepped into the first room. The walls had pink-and-blue bear paper! Baby paper! Sam was a baby! No one had thought of that!

Slam! The door swung shut. Flora ran to open it. There was no knob!

There was only a round hole with a metal bar across it. She put her finger in the hole and tugged on the bar, but the door was stuck. Flora peered through the hole. Flapjack was on the other side. He barked and wagged his tail.

"Dumb dog," said Flora. "Now we're both in big trouble."

Flora pushed the door. She pulled the door. It still wouldn't open.

She went to the window. Dad's car wasn't in the driveway yet. Mom and Polly were in the house. There was no sign of Max or anyone else on Tower Road. "Super big trouble," said Flora.

She looked in the closet. There was a piece of paper on the floor. It said, WET PAINT. Flora wished she had a pencil so she could write a note. Flapjack could take the note home, just like Lassie on those old TV programs.

Flora would be saved — saved, but still in big trouble. But there was no pencil for writing.

Flora peered through the hole in the door again. "Go home, Flapjack," she called. "Get Mom."

Flapjack rolled over. He wiggled like a snake on his back.

"Please!" Flora rattled the door. She tried to open the window. She didn't know how to make the latch work. She waved the paper in front of the glass. But there was no one to see it. "Help!" she yelled. No one came. "Blech!" said Flora. She crumpled the paper.

Flapjack barked. He pawed at the door.

Flora crumpled the paper again, closer to the door. The paper sounded like the wrapping on a cookie package. Flapjack always barked when he thought Flora had cookies. "Come, Flapjack. Get a cookie," said Flora.

Flapjack jumped on the door. He jumped and jumped. Suddenly the door swung open.

"Good dog, Flapjack. Let's go home. Let's get cookies," said Flora.

When Flora got home, she called, "I found Flapjack." But she didn't know if anyone heard her over Polly's crying.

She raced to the kitchen and got three dog biscuits for Flapjack.

"Flora," called Mom. "Come in the family room, please. I need your help *right now*."

Polly was sitting on the couch, her arms folded. Her bottom lip poked way out. "I was just throwing my toys into the box. It's not my fault I'm not a good thrower."

Mom patted Polly's head. "I know

you didn't mean to break the lamp, Polly," she said. "But you have to think before you do things."

"I did think," said Polly. Big tears rolled down her cheeks. "I thinked about picking up my toys as fast as I could."

Mom sighed. "Flora, will you stay with Polly for a few minutes? I have to run next door and ask Sharon Bloom if I can borrow her vacuum. Ours died last week and I haven't had a chance to get it fixed."

"Okay, Mom. Polly, I'll play my Mozart for you," Flora said.

Mom gave Flora a big hug. "Thank you . . . Flora? How did you get paint on your shirt?" she asked.

"Um, I — I — um. In the new house?" Flora said in a whispery voice.

"Flora Ann Cole!" Her mother's

face turned red. "There will be no dessert for one whole week."

"But I had to — I had to get Flapjack," said Flora.

"You should have come home and told me," said her mom.

Flora swallowed her tears. She knew Mom was right. But it was all Flapjack's fault. Why didn't Flapjack get in trouble?

"Now please stay here with Polly," said Mom. "And don't go anywhere . . . don't move! Either of you!"

Flora nodded.

Polly looked at Flora with wide eyes. "Um, I don't want to hear any nose-art. I already heard it seventy-twenty times," she said. "Will you make up a play instead?" asked Polly. "I like your plays better than nose-art."

"It's Mmmm-Mozart, not nose-art,

63

Polly. But okay," said Flora, "we'll do a play instead. The name of this play is *Secret Agent Angelina and Her Spy Dog.* I'll be the secret agent. You can be the bad guy."

"Noooo," wailed Polly. "I don't want to be bad. I want to be the spy dog."

Flora sighed. "Okay. But the only thing you'll get to say is *woof.*"

"No," said Polly. "This spy dog can talk, too. It can say 'I smell a bad guy.'"

"I'm making up this play," said Flora. "The spy dog can't talk."

"Yes it can," said Polly. "The dog is my part."

"Polly, if you keep talking, the play won't start," said Flora.

"Okay," said Polly. She put her finger to her lips. "The spy dog says *woof* and *arf-arf* and *bow-wow* and I smell a bad guy," she whispered.

Flora wrinkled her nose at her sister. Then she began: "Our play takes place far, far away in a big city. In a tiny old house, there lives a very, very brave secret agent named Angelina. She has just had a phone call." Flora pretended to hold a telephone. Then she pretended to hang it up. "Someone needs help," she said. She paced back and forth with her hands behind her back.

"You're not . . . 'posed to move, Flora. Mom said," warned Polly.

"I'm not moving, I'm acting," said Flora.

"Okay," said Polly.

Flora looked around. "Here, Flapjack. Come. We have a new case to solve."

"Flapjack is our dog's name," said Polly. "Angelina should call her dog Sniffer. That is the bestest name for a spy dog."

"Okay," said Flora. "Here, Sniffer." She pointed at her sister. "Now you say *woof.*"

"*Woof.* What do you want? Do you want me to find bad guys?" said Polly.

"Polly! You were only supposed to say *woof.* I didn't ask you to find bad guys yet."

"I know, but you're going to, aren't you? Maybe the spy dog should be called Fluffy. I'd like to be Fluffy. I want to wear a sparkly diamond collar."

"Never mind," said Flora. "The bad guy just got away."

"Uh-oh," said Polly. "He's hiding. Fluffy the spy dog knows where."

"Who's making up this play?" asked Flora, her hands on her hips.

"Oh, oh," said Polly. "The bad guy took Fluffy's diamond collar. Fluffy is sad." She whined like a puppy.

"Stop!" shouted Flora. "Come back with that collar." She ran toward the door as if she were chasing a bad guy.

"*Arf-arf,*" said Polly. She crawled across the floor and pretended to bite Flora.

Flora and Polly were wrestling when Mom came back with the vacuum cleaner.

They both got sent to their room.

Chapter Seven
Flora's Club

All Friday at school, Flora thought about telling Max about Sam. She thought while she and Josie played princess on the playground. She thought while she wrote an ad for Smiley Fudge, candy that won't give you cavities ever.

Now, on Saturday morning, she sat on her front-porch swing. She had written another ad, for Best Friend Baby-sitters. Maybe she could baby-sit for Sam. She had a lot of experience with Polly. She wondered if her mom would let her. She wondered if Sam's mom would hire her.

Polly skipped up the walk. She trailed her jump rope like a tail. "Watch me jump," she said. She held both ends of the rope. "One, two, three," she counted. Then Polly flipped the rope over her head and jumped.

"That's not how you do it," said Flora.

"Yes, it is," said Polly. "That's how I do it." She climbed up beside Flora on the swing. "Want to make another play about Secret Spy Angelina and her spy dog, Fluffy?"

Flora closed her notebook. "Not now. I'm thinking."

Polly swung her feet, making the swing rock. "What are you thinking about?"

Flora sighed. Sometimes Dad said Polly was a question box. Dad was right. "I'm thinking about starting a club," said Flora.

Polly wiggled her jump rope like a snake. "Can I be in your club?"

"No," said Flora.

"Why?" asked Polly. She slid off the swing. She wiggled the rope around Flora's feet. "My pet snake will eat you," she said.

"That's not a pet snake. It's a jump rope," said Flora.

"Uh-huh. It's a jump rope snake." Polly giggled. "I want to be in your club, Flora. Please."

"No. You can't be in my club," said Flora. Polly was such a pest.

"Why?" Polly wiggled her jump rope faster.

Flora looked down at her arm. "Because you have to count your freckles to get in my club."

"I can count my freckles." Polly put

her face right up to Flora's. "See? Lots of freckles. One, two, three, four. On my nose. Mama says they're sun kisses." She puckered her lips as if she were going to kiss Flora.

Flora covered her face. "You have to count *all* your freckles. And be in third grade," she said through her fingers.

"Oh," said Polly. She hopped down the steps. "My friend Lizbeth and I are going to have a Jump Rope Club. You have to jump only my way to be in it." She twirled the jump rope, jumped up and down, and got tangled up.

Flora laughed. Polly stuck out her tongue. "*And you have to be in kindergarten,*" she shouted. "And you have to know how to tap dance — and you don't know how," she said. Polly ran up the steps and into the house.

Flapjack slipped out the door as

Polly went in. He jumped up on the swing and put his head in Flora's lap. Flora petted Flapjack. Flapjack's tail thumped on the wood swing. "Want to be in my club?" Flora asked Flapjack.

Flapjack's tail thumped harder. Flapjack would be in third grade, if he weren't a dog, of course.

"You have to count your freckles to be in my club," Flora said.

Flapjack barked. He had three brown freckles on his nose.

Flora started to count the freckles on her arm. She counted and counted. Flora decided she had one zillion freckles. She looked up from counting as Max came across the lawn.

"Hey, Flora," said Max. "What's happening?"

"I'm starting my club today," she said.

Max sprawled on the porch step.

"Not that dumb Reading Club," he said.

"No. The Freckle Club," said Flora. "Want to join?"

"That sounds pretty dumb, too," said Max. "What do I have to do?"

"Count your freckles. And be in third grade," said Flora.

Max tried to look at his nose. "I can't see my freckles." His eyes crossed.

"I can." Flora plopped down on the porch step. She stared at Max's nose. "You have eleven freckles," she said. "You can be in my Freckle Club. Now we have three members."

"Three?" said Max. "You and me and who else?"

"Flapjack," said Flora. "He has three freckles."

"What does the Freckle Club do, anyway?" asked Max.

Flora sighed. She thought quickly. "We're friends," she said. "No matter what. Third-grade friends who count freckles."

"But what do we *do*?"

"Lots of stuff," said Flora. "It's a freckle-counting, making-stuff . . ."

Max wrinkled up his nose. "Making-stuff?"

"Sort of Sports Club," added Flora quickly.

"But mostly sports," said Max. "Right, Flora?"

Flora shrugged.

"I know," said Max. "We need a secret password. "It could be . . . SCORE."

"That's too easy," said Flora.

"Then how about secret names?" said Max. "Mine will be Babe."

"Like the pig?" asked Flora.

"Pig? What pig? After the great Babe Ruth, the baseball player."

"Secret names are too confusing. How about secret numbers? The number of our freckles," said Flora.

"I guess. I'm number eleven," said Max.

"Flapjack is three. I'm number one zillion," said Flora.

"Zowie!" said Max. "That's a lot of freckles. So, let's play kickball now."

"Flora, honey, I need you," called her mom.

"I have to go," Flora said. "Meet here later for a Freckle-Sports Club meeting. Okay?"

"Okay," said Max. He ran down the front walk. "Wait till I tell the guys. They'll all want to be in our Sports Club."

Flora waved. "It's a Freckle Club," she said as she opened the porch door. And she didn't want Max to tell the guys. This wasn't working out right.

She had to think. What does a Freckle Club do, besides count freckles and be friends?

Flora thought about it while she practiced piano. She thought about it while she helped Mom fold laundry. She thought about it while she put away the toys in the family room. And she thought about it while she brushed Flapjack. Flora thought and thought and she still couldn't think of any good Freckle Club things to do. But she did get an idea for a club poem.

After Flora finished working on the Freckle Club poem, she turned to her GOOD-BAD list.

9) GOOD — Having a Freckle Club with Max and Flapjack.

10) BAD — Having a Sports Club with Max and all the boys he'll want to invite to join.

Chapter Eight
The First Meeting

After lunch, Flora called Max to come over. The first Freckle Club meeting was in Flora's room.

"Eleven here," said Max.

"One zillion here," said Flora. "Three is sleeping. He can't come today," she said.

"They're putting blue carpet in the new house," said Max. "Want to go watch?" He ran to the window to look out.

"No. We're having a meeting," said Flora. "I made up a secret chant. It goes like this." She'd decided to call it a club chant instead of a poem. She knew Max would say "eee-yew" if she wanted to have a club poem. Flora opened her notebook. She took a deep breath.

Spend a penny; guess how many
Fifty freckles on my nose
Fifty freckles on my toes
Millions, billions, trillions, zillions
Period!

Flora clapped her hands and shouted the last word. "We'll say this at every meeting. You try it."

Max said the chant after Flora, but not very loud. "It sounds like a poem. How come it's not about sports, like soccer and baseball?"

"I made it rhyme so it would be easy to remember," said Flora. "And nothing rhymes with soccer or base-ball!"

"Oh, okay," said Max. "Now let's go to the new house."

"No. We have to make a list of stuff our club will do," Flora said.

"Like what?" asked Max. "We're just going to play sports."

"That's not a club. We need to do other stuff, too. Like helping neigh-bors. We could rake leaves," said Flora.

"Not till they fall off the trees," said Max.

"We could walk dogs," said Flora.

"You're the only one who has one," said Max.

"We could make a list of good stuff about living on Tower Road — for the new people," said Flora. "Where the ice cream store is and where the li-brary is and where the market is and . . ."

"And where the park where we play soccer is and where the pet store is," Max said. "Sam will want to know that stuff. Won't he?"

Flora smiled. No he won't, she thought. But she didn't tell what she knew about Sam. Max wouldn't want to make the list if he knew Sam was a baby.

"And how to call the police and the fire department," said Max. "I can get a phone sticker from my brother." His brother was a firefighter.

"We could draw a map of the neighborhood," said Flora. "It could say WELCOME FROM THE FRECKLE CLUB at the top."

"From the Freckle-Sports Club," said Max.

"We're here." Polly skipped into the room with her friend Lizbeth. "What are you doing?" Polly asked.

"Get out right this minute, Polly," said Flora. "We're having a Freckle Club meeting."

"I don't have to get out. This is my room, too," said Polly. "Lizbeth and I are going to have a Jump Rope Club meeting. Huh, Lizbeth?"

Lizbeth nodded. She and Polly sat on the floor by Flora.

"I'm telling Mom," said Flora.

"Come on, Lizbeth. I'll show you our new computer soccer game," said Polly.

"Computer soccer!" Max ran to the desk. "Let me see."

Polly booted up the computer.

"Way cool," said Max. This was the first time Flora had seen Max so excited about anything.

"But what about our club meeting?" asked Flora.

"Oh, we don't have a real club yet,"

said Max. "Polly, can I play the game?" he asked.

Polly slid over on the chair. "First you have to pick how fast you want to play," she said.

"Yes, we do have a real club," said Flora.

"We don't even have a clubhouse," said Max. "How can you have a club without a clubhouse?"

"Members make clubs, not a clubhouse." Flora tried not to cry as she left her room. Behind her she could hear Max shouting. She heard Polly laughing. Even Lizbeth was cheering for Max.

Flora passed the kitchen where Mom was sharing some string cheese with Flapjack. She didn't feel like talking, so she headed for the backyard where the willow tree grew. As she slipped between the branches, big wet tears slid down her freckled cheeks. She sat against the trunk.

Everything was BAD-BAD-BAD.

Minutes later, Flapjack pushed at Flora's arm. He licked away her tears.

"You like me, huh, Flapjack? You're my friend." She kissed Flapjack on the top of the head. "And I like you best of anyone."

Flapjack rested his head in Flora's lap.

"Do you think our club is dumb?" Flora asked.

Flapjack *woof*ed.

"That means no," Flora said. She stroked Flapjack. If only Sam were a girl. Then they could have a really good club. They wouldn't have to ask any boys to belong if they didn't want to.

The boys could belong to Polly's dumb Jump Rope Club. They could

play sports all day. Flora wouldn't care one freckle's worth. She didn't know how to play soccer or baseball and she didn't want to learn.

"But Sam is a baby boy," said Flora. "So I need a real clubhouse if I want to have a club."

She looked around. "Maybe we could meet under this tree," she said. "At least until it gets too cold. The Freckle Club is a really good idea," she told Flapjack, who yawned. "Yes! When we have meetings, my willow tree will be the clubhouse." It wasn't a great idea, she knew. But she hoped it would do. She'd try to convince Max that the willow would make the perfect clubhouse. She headed back to her room. She'd give Max one more chance. One more and that was all.

When she got to her room, Polly

and Lizbeth were playing computer soccer.

"Where's Max?" Flora asked.

"He left," said Polly.

"Blech!" said Flora. Nothing was working out right.

Chapter Nine
Moving Day

The next week at school, Flora, Trang, and Josie had fun working on their magazine ads. Trang drew a picture of a soccer player. He wrote:

Even in the winter, you can play computer soccer.
Find this and other games at Trang's Computer Corner.

"It's my favorite game," he said.
"Not mine," said Josie. "I have a game called Fairyland."

"Me, too!" said Flora. "It's my favorite."

"Mine, too," said Josie. "Want to come to my house and play it sometime?"

"Okay," said Flora. "I'll ask my mom." Josie was acting like a real friend. Flora smiled as she looked at Josie. She had lots of freckles like Flora. Would Josie like to be in her Freckle Club? Flora wondered. She would have to talk to Max first. They had never talked about the rules for new members. And if she asked Josie, he might want to ask all those boys.

"Get busy, students," said Mrs. Lee. "We don't have extra time for our project today."

Flora knew why. They were going to start times tables today. She hoped they wouldn't be hard.

"Look at Josie's ad," said Trang.

Josie showed how she'd used black art paper to make tap shoes. She'd used sparkle glue to make the ribbons. "I just have to make the printing," she said.

Flora read the classified ads she'd written. They liked the one for the lost dog and the baby-sitter one the best. All she had to do was her big ad for the bookstore.

"This group is doing a fine job," said Mrs. Lee when she checked on them.

"It's not fair, Mrs. Lee," Kate called. She didn't even raise her hand. "The Kool Duds Kid isn't even in school. My team has only two people."

It was true. Samantha Gold had not come back to school since the first day.

"She will be back next week," said Mrs. Lee. "You and Adam continue to work on your part of the project,

Kate," she said. "Your other team member will catch up."

Kate sighed really loud.

"It isn't fair," said Josie.

Flora raised her hand. "Mrs. Lee, when our team is finished, we could help Kate's team," she said.

"No," said Kate. "I don't want your help."

"Thank you for offering, Flora," said Mrs. Lee.

Flora brought her hand down. No matter what she tried, Kate got angry. Well, she wouldn't try anymore.

"Don't be mad at her," whispered Josie.

"Why not?" asked Flora.

Josie looked over at Kate. "I can't tell you," she said.

What couldn't Josie tell her? Flora tried and tried to find out. But Josie was really good at keeping a secret.

Flora knew that was a good thing. But she still wished she knew what Kate's secret was.

The week passed quickly. It was Saturday morning when Max pounded on Flora's front door. "Flora, come outside," he called.

Flora ran downstairs. She hadn't even had breakfast yet. She pushed open the screen door.

"I ran here as fast as I could," Max panted. "We have to have a club meeting right now!"

"Why?" Flora asked.

"Because my mom found out that the new people are moving in this afternoon. We have to finish our list. We have to make a map for them."

"Okay. Meet me under the willow tree in five minutes. The willow is our clubhouse."

"Cool! I'll wait for you." He jumped from the top porch step.

"Come to breakfast," Mom called.

Mom and Dad were already at the table. Usually Dad read the paper at breakfast. But not today.

"Like third grade any better?" he asked.

Flora smiled and nodded. She kept eating.

"How's the magazine project coming?"

Flora nodded and ate faster.

Finally the last question. "You want to leave the table, Flora Belle?"

Flora smiled and nodded. She stuffed in her last bite of French toast.

"Have fun," Dad said as she pushed in her chair.

"Brush your teeth and comb your

hair first," Mom said. "And make your bed."

"But Polly didn't make her bed," Flora complained.

"Flora," said Mom, "right now Polly is sleeping in her bed."

Dad dished up more French toast for Mom. "Listen to your mom," he said.

Flora sighed. She bet when her sister got up, she still wouldn't have to make her bed. Polly never had to do as much as Flora.

At last she could go to the meeting. She took a big pad of paper and some colored markers. Max was waiting. He was eating a slice of toast and had jelly on his face. "I brought a rug," he said.

"Thanks. That was a good idea," she said. Maybe boys weren't as bad as she thought. Flora put the pad of paper down on the rug and lay on her stomach. "You be in charge of drawing. I'll be in charge of writing," she said. "First draw the new people's house."

"Why?" asked Max. "They know where their house is."

"Well, if they go to the store or something, they might not know how to get back. They could get lost. Besides, a picture will show it's important," said Flora.

"I can draw their house. And my house," said Max.

"My house is important, too," said Flora, opening the markers.

"What about our clubhouse here?" asked Max. "We're going to ask Sam to join our club, aren't we?" He was already sketching.

"Let's wait until Sam gets here," said Flora, smiling. "Then we can decide." She printed SAM'S HOUSE on the map, while Max drew trees in the park and started drawing his own house.

They worked for a while. The markers sometimes squeaked as they pulled across the paper. Occasionally a willow leaf dropped onto the map. Flora blew them off.

Finally Max stood up. He looked down at the map. "We need our school. And what about the gas station?"

"Dads always know how to find gas stations," said Flora. "Besides, we don't know which one to put in."

"But we put in all the churches," said Max. "And what if Sam doesn't have a dad?" He sighed.

"The map is getting crowded," said Flora. "But you're right. Put in the gas stations."

Flora was printing A WELCOME MAP when she heard the squeal of truck brakes.

Max dropped his marker. "They're here. Come on, Flora."

All morning, Flora and Max sat on the curb watching. The moving men walked in and out of the truck over and over. Flora saw a lot of furniture and a lot of boxes. But so far no new people had come.

Before lunch, they went back to the willow tree. Max and Flora finished the map, stopping now and then to check if the new people had come. Flora liked the way the map looked. She thought she might use a map in her next play.

After lunch, Mom called to Flora. "It's time for Polly's dance lesson," she said. "Come on, Flora."

"Please. Let me stay here. I don't

want to miss the new people," she said.

"The new people will be living here for a long time," said Mom. "Your dad had to go into work and you can't stay alone," she said.

"I'll give them the map," said Max. "I'll tell them you helped."

"No. Please. Wait until I come back," said Flora. "Please."

"Do I have to?" asked Max. He made a long face.

Flora made a long face back.

"Oh, okay," said Max. "You go to tappy-tap dancy-dance with your mom." He laughed at his own silly joke. "Besides, they aren't even here yet."

"Thanks," said Flora. She ran to the car. She wished she didn't have to go to stupid tap class with Polly.

At the Little Swan Dance School,

Mom and Flora sat on wooden chairs at the side of the room. "You watch Polly dance. I'm going to run to the drugstore. I'll be back in a few minutes," said Mom.

Flora made a grouchy face. She swung her feet as she watched Polly flap her arms and *clickity-clack* across the floor. Flora wanted to go home. She wondered if the new people had come. She wondered if Max knew now that Sam was a baby. That made Flora smile.

Chapter Ten
The New People

When Mom pulled into the drive, Flora was the first one out of the car. Polly had gone home with Lizbeth, so she wasn't with them.

Max was still by the curb. He was bouncing a basketball. The moving truck was gone.

"Did they come yet?" asked Flora. She crossed her fingers for luck.

"Not yet," said Max. He made the ball bounce really high and ran to catch it. "They're never going to move in. We'll be waiting here until we are a hundred years old, watching for the new people. We hurried to make our map for nothing."

"Do the new people have nice furniture? Does Sam have a lot of toys?" asked Flora, smiling.

Max put his foot on the basketball. He shrugged. "Sam's family has three bikes," he said. "I didn't look at the furniture. And all his toys must be in boxes. I saw a black piano and a giant screen TV. I can't wait to see baseball on that TV."

"What kind of bed does Sam have?" Flora asked, swallowing a smile.

Max looked puzzled. "Just a bed, I guess. I didn't see it. Maybe it came when I went home for a snack."

"Oh," said Flora. He didn't know about Sam yet.

As she settled on the curb, a white

van came down the street. It pulled into the driveway of the new house. A lady and a man with a camera got out.

"Smile, kids," said the man.

Click! Click! Click! went the camera.

"Why did he take our picture?" asked Max.

"I don't know," said Flora.

The man took pictures of the new house. He took pictures of the van.

The lady ran up to the porch. She wore a long purple dress. Purple earrings dangled from her ears. "Come on, Sam," she called.

Max gave Flora a high-five hand slap. "He's here," said Max.

"Where?" Flora asked. She didn't see a baby. She only saw grown-ups.

The lady and man went inside.

"Maybe he went inside already," said Max.

"No, he didn't," said Flora. "I was watching every minute."

"Go ring the bell and ask," said Max.

"You go," said Flora.

"Not me," said Max.

Flora sighed. She hurried across the street. Near the van, she heard *THUMM! THUMM! THUMM!*

On tiptoe Flora peeked in the window. Someone was sitting in the back of the van playing a big violin, the kind that was too big to put under your chin.

"Sam, you can practice your cello later." The lady came out of the house. "Hi, honey," she said to Flora.

"Hi," said Flora. Up close she could see that the lady was going to have a baby. So Sam wasn't the baby, after all. Sam was another BOY! "Blech," muttered Flora.

104

The lady opened the van door. "Samantha Rose Gold, this is your mother speaking. Read my lips. Get out of that van. Now."

The girl got out. She wore purple shorts and a purple shirt and purple knee pads. She folded her arms. "I am out," she said.

Flora couldn't stop staring. "You . . . you're . . . you are the Kool Duds Kid!" she said.

"Yeah? So what?" said Sam.

GOOD — Sam was a girl. . . .

BAD — Sam was the Kool Duds Kid.

Blech! Blech! Blech!

Chapter Eleven
D-U-M-B

Mrs. Gold tucked in Sam's shirt. "You gotta make Kool Duds look good, kiddo. That's your job," she said. She ran back to the house.

"I hate Kool Duds," said Sam. She untucked her shirt. "Everything in my life is purple. Everywhere I look — Kool Duds. I can't pick out even one thing that I'd like to wear. I want to wear something black! Kool Duds are D-U-M-B."

"You are Sam," said Flora. She stared at the new girl. She felt

D-U-M-B, too. Polly had been right. Girls could have boys' names. And she'd never even thought of Samantha as being Sam.

"That's my name. Don't wear it out," said Sam.

Flora waved to Max. "Remember me? I'm Flora Cole. I sit across from you in Mrs. Lee's room. And this is Max Bloom." Flora turned to Max. "And this . . . this is Sam Gold."

"You can't be Sam," said Max.

"Don't bet on it," said Sam.

"Gee," said Flora. Sam sounded like Kate.

"Oh," said Max. "Are you really Sam?"

"Yeah. Really. So what?" said Sam.

"Her name is really Samantha and she's in my class at school," said Flora. "Where have you been?"

"Samantha is just my school

name," said Sam. "And I've been working. When I work, I have a tutor."

"You're supposed to be a boy," said Max.

"No I'm not," said Sam.

"He thought you were," said Flora. "But I'm glad you're not. We need more girls on this street."

"No we don't," said Max.

"Invite your new friends inside, Sam," called her mother.

Sam stared at Flora and Max. No one said anything.

"Let's go home," said Max. He bounced the basketball.

"Sam plays the cello," said Flora. She didn't want to go yet.

"I'm going to be in an orchestra someday," said Sam.

"Me, too," said Flora. "I play the pi-ano."

"Well, I play soccer, baseball, basketball, and lots of other sports," said Max.

"Why are boys so D-U-M-B?" asked Sam.

"Girls are the D-U-M-B ones," said Max. He bounced the ball higher.

"Don't bet on it," said Sam. She grabbed the ball as it came down. She ran into her house and slammed the door.

"Hey!" shouted Max.

"Sam!" shouted Flora.

"It's all your fault," Max shouted at Flora. "You have to get my ball."

"Me?" said Flora. "I didn't do anything."

"*You* talked to her," said Max.

"So did you," said Flora.

"She's a girl," said Max. "And she's in your class. You have to go. I'll wait here." He sat on the curb.

Flora edged up the walk. She remembered the last time she'd been in

Sam's house. Sam's house meant trouble. She stepped on the porch. The front door opened.

"Hold it, kid!" said the man with the camera. *Click! Click!*

"Stop it, Dave," said Sam.

Flora didn't know anyone who called their dad by his first name.

"It's my job, Sammy." Dave took her picture, too.

Sam glared at him.

Flora looked around. Furniture was sitting every which way. Boxes were stacked everywhere. The house didn't look as big with all the stuff inside. "You have a nice house," said Flora.

"Not as nice as our old one in our old town," said Sam. "All my *wonderful best friends* live there."

"You'll like it here, too," said Flora.

"Everyone is waiting for you to come back to school."

"Right. Like I believe you. They are waiting for the Kool Duds Kid, not me," said Sam. "So what do you want?"

"The basketball, please," said Flora.

"Here." Sam pushed the ball at Flora.

"Do you want to play?" asked Flora.

"No," said Sam.

"Oh," said Flora.

"Good-bye," said Sam.

"Bye," said Flora. She stepped out the door. She looked back at Sam.

"Now what?" asked Sam.

"Do you want to join our club?" asked Flora.

"D-U-M-B. Do I act like I want to?" asked Sam.

"No," said Flora. "But maybe you'd like it," she said.

"Don't bet on it," said Sam. She slammed the door.

"Blech!" said Flora. She carried the ball to Max.

"See you later," he said.

"What about the map and the list?" asked Flora. "When are we going to give it to the new people?"

"We're not," said Max. "Sam's weird. Who cares if she gets lost. She's just like Kate, who was in my class last year."

"Kate? You know Kate?" said Flora.

"I hate Kate," said Max. "I'm glad she's not in my class and I'm glad she's moving away. She wasn't even supposed to be back at school this year. My mom said they just sold their house."

"Oh," said Flora. "I bet Kate's

scared of being a new kid. And I bet Sam is, too."

"Are new kids scared?" asked Max.

Flora nodded.

Max shrugged. "I wouldn't be scared. The kids at Poplar are nice."

"You don't know that when you are new. You don't know anyone," said Flora.

"Well, you know me," said Max.

"But not at school. You didn't even say hi when I said hi," she said.

Max kicked the ground with his toe. "Oh," he said. "The other kids tease . . ."

"I know," said Flora. "Now there's Sam. And she doesn't even know you. Maybe she's scared." Flora didn't like remembering what it was like being the new kid.

"Maybe," said Max. "But I don't want to go back there now. She *scares* me, just like Kate."

"Did I scare you?" asked Flora.

"Nah," said Max. "But I was afraid you'd only want to do school stuff and girl stuff all the time."

"Oh," said Flora. She'd never thought that boys could be afraid, too.

"Maybe we'll go back tomorrow," said Max.

"Okay," said Flora. "Tomorrow." She looked back at Sam's house.

Sam was standing in the upstairs window. In the same room Flora had gotten stuck in. Sam was looking at Flora.

Flora started to wave, then changed her mind. Trouble, thought Flora. The new house was trouble. And Sam was trouble. Kate might be moving away. But Sam was moving in. She wasn't sure if this was a GOOD thing or a BAD thing. But it was looking more BAD than GOOD.

Chapter Twelve
Sam, Kate, and *Three*

Flora had been in front waiting to go to church when the Golds left their house the next morning. She waved.

Sam just looked out the van window without waving back.

"I told you Sam would be a girl," said Polly. She hopped in circles. She flapped her arms like a D-U-M-B baby bird.

Flora started to make a face but changed her mind when Mom came out the front door.

After church, Flora and Max waited

on the curb all afternoon. The Golds didn't come back.

On Monday, when Flora got to school, Josie ran to meet her.

"Guess what?" they both said at the same time.

"What?" asked Flora. "You first."

"Kate moved. She's not coming back to Poplar."

"Where did she go?" asked Flora. One more GOOD thing for her list!

"I think to Minnesota where her grandma lives," said Josie. "Her mom and dad got a divorce." Josie looked down at her tennies. "No one wanted Kate."

"No one? What do you mean?" asked Flora.

"Her dad left last year. Kate made us promise not to tell. Then her mom said as soon as the house was sold, Kate would have to go live with her

118

grandma." Josie sighed. "My mom says that's why she's been so mad and so mean to everyone. Meg and I were hoping they'd never sell her house."

"I'm sorry we couldn't be friends," said Flora. But she wasn't sad that Kate was gone. She didn't think Kate would ever have wanted to be her friend.

"I'll ask my mom to get Kate's new address. We could write to her," said Josie.

"Even me?" asked Flora.

"Of course, even you," said Josie.

"And we could send her a copy of *Three,* our magazine," said Flora.

"Yeah," said Josie. "We could do that."

They ran across the playground and into school.

"I almost forgot. What was your news?" asked Josie.

"Oh! You know the Kool Duds Kid, Samantha Gold?" said Flora.

"Yeah. What about her?" asked Josie.

"She moved across the street from me," said Flora.

"Luck-y!" said Josie.

"Don't bet on it," said Flora.

"Why? What's she like?" asked Josie.

"You know. Same as at school. She's not so nice," said Flora.

"So, where is she?" asked Josie as they entered the classroom.

Flora looked around. "I don't know," she said. "Maybe she's making an ad today."

"I wonder if that's fun," said Josie. "Do you think she'd tell us?"

"Maybe," said Flora. She wasn't sure what Sam would do.

Sam came into the classroom just

as the bell rang. She plopped into the seat across from Flora, but she didn't say anything. Today she was wearing different purple Kool Duds.

Sam was a good reader. She knew cursive. She knew up to the four times tables already.

When it was time to work on *Three,* Mrs. Lee made an announcement.

"I'm sorry to say that Kate has moved. She won't be coming back to Poplar Elementary. Samantha, you were going to be on Adam and Kate's team. But you are getting a late start. So instead, you and Adam will be the editors for *Three*. That means you'll collect all the parts. Go over them with me. Arrange them in order. And be responsible for the magazine cover."

"What about the stuff Kate and I wrote?" asked Adam.

"It will still be used," said Mrs. Lee.

Flora sighed. She had hoped she'd get picked to be the editor. Now, because Kate was gone, Sam got the best job.

"Gee, they have a lot to do," said Josie. "I'm glad we're almost finished with our part."

Flora nodded. Maybe Josie was right. Still, she wished she could have been an editor.

Mrs. Lee collected the magazine parts that each team had done.

Flora really liked doing the project. It was fun. Then she had an idea. The Freckle Club could have a magazine. Why not? Because . . . Max wouldn't want to. I have so many good ideas, she thought. If only Max thought so, too.

At lunchtime, Flora sat with Josie. Flora was surprised when Meg asked to sit with them, too. And she was even more surprised when Josie asked if it was okay. "Sure, that would be nice," said Flora. "We aren't having tuna surprise, are we?" Josie and Meg laughed at Flora's joke.

Samantha was the last one to come into the lunchroom. She looked around.

Flora remembered her first day as the new kid. She went to get Sam.

"Come and sit with us, Sam," she said. She pointed to the table.

"I can't," said Sam. "I'm not eating at school. I just wanted to see . . ."

"Why?" asked Flora.

"My mom is picking me up. I have to reshoot part of the Kool Duds ad this afternoon," said Sam.

"Oh," said Flora. "See ya."

"Yeah. See ya," said Sam. She ran from the cafeteria.

"Where's she going?" asked Meg.

"To wait for her mom. She has to do a Kool Duds ad today," said Flora.

"Oh, big deal," said Meg. "Did she want to give you her autograph?"

Meg and Josie laughed.

"Don't," said Flora. "It's hard to be a new kid. If she were Kate, you would be nice." Even if Kate wasn't the Kool Duds Kid, she thought. Why didn't I think of that before? "I think it's harder for Sam to be new because she *is* the Kool Duds Kid."

"Yeah, maybe. But I still wish she was Kate," said Meg.

Flora sipped her milk. She didn't want to be mean, but she knew she was glad Kate was gone. And even after what she said, she still wasn't so sure she was glad Sam had come.

Chapter Thirteen
Not One Freckle

After school, Flora made up a symphony at the piano while she waited for Max to come for their meeting. They had to decide what to do about the list and the map they'd made for the Golds. Flora was going over her GOOD-BAD list. She was surprised. Some of the BAD things were not so BAD anymore.

Max slipped into their clubhouse space under the willow tree. He was clutching a soccer ball. "She's out there," he whispered.

Flapjack looked up, then rested his

head on his paws. He didn't even bark at Max. Flora guessed he was used to living on Tower Road now. He was used to Max, too.

Flora closed her notebook and peeked between the branches.

"She's just walking around in front," said Max. "I think she stole some kid's Hacky-Sack."

"Maybe she wants to be in our club," said Flora.

"Well, we don't want her to be," said Max.

"Well, maybe I do," said Flora.

"Why?" asked Max.

"Hello, my little bluebirds." Polly's head poked between the branches on the other side of the tree. "Can I come in your clubhouse, Flora?" she asked.

"She's not a member," said Max.

"Not now," said Flora. "We're having a club meeting."

Polly stepped through the branches anyway. Sam pushed in right behind her.

"Who said she could come in here?" asked Max, pointing to Sam. He sat on his soccer ball. "This is a private club."

Flapjack wagged his tail as Polly petted him.

"Who cares?" said Sam. She turned to leave.

"Wait," said Flora. "You can stay for a little while. If you want to."

"Can I stay, too?" asked Polly.

"Flora!" said Max. "We didn't vote. I vote no."

"I vote yes," said Polly.

"You can't vote," said Max.

"I vote yes, too," said Flora. "And so does Flapjack."

"*Woof,*" said Flapjack.

"That's a yes. So it's two to one," said Flora. "Anyway, I win because I'm the president."

"Who said you're the president?" asked Max. "I never said that."

"Never mind. I vote no," said Sam. She left.

"She's nice," said Polly. She ran after Sam.

"Flora, what did you do that for?" asked Max. "She's not nice. She took my basketball. Remember?"

"We need another girl in our club," said Flora.

"No we don't," said Max.

"Yes we do," said Flora. "You and Flapjack are both boys. We need a girl to make it even."

"Okay, Polly can be in the club," said Max.

"No *she* can't!" said Flora. "Polly is

in kindergarten. You have to be in third grade — like Sam." Flora left, too.

"I quit," Max shouted after her. "I quit your dumb Sports Club."

"It's a Freckle Club," Flora shouted. "MY FRECKLE CLUB!" She raced down the drive. Max passed her, heading home.

Across the street Sam sat on her porch with her cello. Polly was with her kicking the Hacky-Sack, then running to get it. Flora walked fast to the new house. She sat beside Sam. She waited.

"Go away," said Sam. *THRUMM, THRUMM, THRUMM.* She pulled a long bow over the cello strings. "This is my private porch and I'm practicing."

Polly made tiptoe circles across the porch. She flapped her arms. She stood on one leg. She shuffled her feet. "I'm practicing, too," she said. "Miss Marcy said I should. Do you want to be a worm, Flora?" she asked.

"No," said Flora. She turned to Sam. "What's the matter with you?" she asked.

"Nothing," said Sam.

"Are you always so mean?" asked Flora.

"Are you always so nosy?" asked Sam.

"I guess so," said Flora. She got up to go. "Come on, Polly. You have to come home."

"No I don't," said Polly.

"Yes you do," said Flora. "You have to come home right now."

"Wait!" said Sam.

"Why?" said Flora.

"I'm sorry — sort of," said Sam.

Flora turned back. "Me, too — sort

of," said Flora. "I thought we could be friends."

Sam started to play her cello again. "I guess not," she said. "I'm too mean. So you don't like me."

"No you're not," said Polly. "Flora is mean sometimes. And I still like her." She sat between Sam and Flora.

"I don't mean to be mean to you, Polly," said Flora.

"I didn't mean it, either," said Sam. "I just don't like being the new kid."

"It's not so bad. Polly and I were new kids at the beginning of summer," said Flora.

"Yeah, but you don't have to wear Kool Duds. You don't have to leave school for shoots. Everyone is always looking at me. They all think I'm stuck-up," said Sam. "And they don't even know me."

"What's stuck-up?" asked Polly. "Is it like glue?"

"No," said Flora. "It's thinking you are better than everyone else."

"Oh. Sam isn't better," said Polly. "I told you, she's nice."

"You're nice, too, Polly," said Sam.

Polly smiled. She took Flora's hand and Sam's hand. "We are all the bestest," she said. "Betterer and bestest."

"Sam, don't you want to be in my club?" Flora asked.

"I guess so," said Sam. "If you want me."

"Good. Come back to my house then," said Flora.

Sam put her cello inside. She took Polly's hand. Flora, Sam, and Polly crossed the street.

"I have to go to the bathroom," said

Polly. She ran up the porch steps. Sam and Flora looked at each other and laughed.

Max was coming from under the willow. "I forgot my rug," he said.

"Wait," said Flora. She grabbed Sam's hand and they ran. "Sam wants to be in our club," she said. "Okay, Max?" asked Flora. "It's okay, isn't it?"

"Don't bet on it," said Max.

"Max, Sam's new. Say yes."

"No!" said Max.

"Why not?" shouted Flora. "Sam is in the third grade."

"I don't like people who steal basketballs and Hacky-Sacks from other people," said Max.

"I gave you back your ball," said Sam. "And the Hacky-Sack is mine. I use it to practice my soccer kicks when I'm shooting commercials."

"Sure you do," said Max. "Girls can't use a Hacky-Sack, anyway. It's too hard for girls."

"Don't bet on it," said Sam. She threw the small leather ball into the air and used her feet and her knees and her head to keep it there.

Max's mouth opened in surprise. "Gee, you're really good with a Hacky-Sack," he said.

"And she is real-ly good at soccer," added Flora. "She was the star of her team at her old school. Weren't you, Sam?"

"Yeah, how did you know that?" asked Sam.

"I guessed," said Flora with a smile.

"I still say N-O," said Max. He bounced his ball off his knee and caught it. "She can't be in our club be-cause of the rule."

"What rule?" asked Sam.

"Yeah, what rule?" asked Flora.

"The freckle rule," said Max. "She doesn't have one single freckle."

"None?" said Flora.

Sam shook her head. "None," she said.

"Nowhere?" asked Flora.

"Nowhere," said Sam.

"Blech," said Flora. This is a real BAD thing, she thought.

Chapter Fourteen
How Many Freckles?

The Freckle-Sports Club — Flora and Max — sat under the willow tree. They stared at Sam.

"Now hold still," said Max. He poked Sam's face with brown eyeliner pencil. It was one of his mom's samples.

"Let me see," said Sam.

Flora held up the mirror.

"I look like I have chicken pox," said Sam, wrinkling her nose.

"You have freckles," said Flora. "Let's count them."

"I made eleven, like me," said Max.

"Give her more," said Flora. "We can't have two elevens." She took the pencil. "Twelve," he said. "Twelve is your secret name, Sam."

"You want to play soccer, Sam?" asked Max.

"Do you like to make bead bracelets?" asked Flora.

"You bet," said Sam. "All of that stuff."

"Way cool!" said Max. "Here," he said. "We made this for you." He handed Sam the list and the map.

Now it was Sam's turn to be surprised. "My mom and Dave will really like this," she said. "Thanks."

Flora smiled. Sam wasn't so bad when you got to know her. The Freckle-Sports Club was going to be so neat. And third grade was going to be better and betterer. Everything was going to be the bestest! In her notebook she'd write:

11) GOOD — The Freckle-Sports Club.

BUT . . .

The next day at school, Sam came over to the fence where Flora, Meg, and Josie were waiting for the bell to ring. Sam's freckles were gone.

"My mother washed them off," said Sam.

"We can make more," said Flora.

"My mother will get mad," said Sam. "She said I'd better not come home with any more stuff on my face. That means I'm not in the club, huh?" She looked as if she were going to cry. "I won't get to make things. Or play soccer."

"Don't worry. We'll have a meeting

right after school," said Flora. "We'll think of something."

"Your club sounds like fun," said Meg.

"Really neat," said Josie. "And we have freckles," she whispered.

Flora smiled. "It would be so much fun for you to be in our club. But . . . I have to ask the other members."

"I think it would be great if they joined," said Sam. "They can have my place."

"No they can't, Sam. You are a member of the club forever. We'll think of something. Then we'll all be members."

Meg and Josie jumped up and down. "Ask today. Please," they said together. "Please."

Flora promised she would. "I'll tell you what Max says tomorrow."

"Max who?" asked Josie.

"Oh, never mind," said Flora.

All the girls started talking at once. And when the bell rang, all four held hands and skipped into class.

"I'm going to write to Kate this afternoon and tell her all about Flora's club," said Josie.

"Neat idea," said Meg.

Flora wondered if they'd want to be part of her club if Kate were still there. She wondered if Kate would have wanted to join. She wondered if she and Max would have said yes.

After school, when Max and Sam came for the meeting, Flora taught Sam the Freckle-Sports Club chant.

Spend a penny; guess how many
Fifty freckles on my nose
Fifty freckles on my toes
Millions, billions, trillions, zillions
Period!

"But what good does it do for me to know it?" asked Sam. "I don't have any freckles. I can't have any freckles. None. Zero. Period!"

"I'll go get the pencil again," said Max. "We'll make the freckles so tiny your mom won't notice."

"She'll notice," said Sam. "Mothers notice everything. Especially my mother."

"My mother, too," said Flora.

"I know," said Max. "Toe freckles. They won't be on your face. I'll get the pen my mom used to mark my camp shirts. If my name won't wash off, your freckles won't wash off, either!" He ducked between the willow branches.

"Let's all have toe freckles," said Flora when Max returned.

Just as they took off their shoes and socks, Polly burst between the

branches. "What are you doing?" she asked.

"Making toe freckles," said Flora.

"Does Mommy know?" asked Polly.

"She won't care," said Flora, trying to sound certain.

"Okay!" said Polly. She raced away.

But Flora was wrong. Mom took the freckles off everyone with nail polish remover. "Draw on paper, not on yourselves," said Mom, while Polly watched.

"Polly, you are such a tattletale. You told about the toe freckles," Flora shouted when Mom had gone back inside. "You'd better not come under this willow tree ever again."

"Okay. Come on, snake," Polly said. She dragged her jump rope behind her.

"Now what?" asked Max. "No freckles. No secret name." He leaned against the tree trunk.

Flora climbed onto a tree branch.

Sam rested against Flapjack on the rug. For a while no one said anything.

"I've got it!" said Flora. "Let's count Sam's freckles."

"We can't," said Max. "Sam has no freckles. None. Not one. Zero."

"So, that's her secret name," said Flora. "Sam's name is Zero. The club rule is that you have to be in third grade and *count* freckles — not *have* freckles."

"Zero sounds real secret. I like that," said Sam.

"Great idea," said Max.

"Let's say our chant," said Flora.

All the members, except Number Three who was now sleeping, recited:

Spend a penny; guess how many
Fifty freckles on my nose
Fifty freckles on my toes

Millions, billions, trillions,
zillions, ZERO!
Period!

Sam held up her hands. Flora clapped hers against Sam's. Then she clapped them against Max's. They laughed.

"Now," said Flora. "I have some really GOOD news. Two more kids want to be in our club."

"Who? Do they have freckles?" asked Max. "Are they in third grade? Are they good at sports?"

"Yes . . . yes . . . and I don't know," said Flora.

"It doesn't matter," said Sam. "Max, at club meetings, you'll help me teach them how to play sports."

"Teach me, too," said Flora.

"All right!" shouted Max and Sam.

"We really do have a Sports Club,"

147

said Max. "Hey! Flora, are the two kids boys? 'Cause I know some boys who want to join, too."

"How many boys?" asked Flora.

"Three," said Max.

"We'll have to vote," said Sam.

"Blech," said Flora, but she really didn't mean it.